THE
MEEK

ISBN 978-0-9981937-0-0 (paperback)
ISBN 978-0-9981937-1-7 (hardcover)

First edition: January 2017
Printed in China
10 9 8 7 6 5 4 3 2 1

This volume collects the first three chapters of the online comic The Meek,
which were published from December 2008–October 2011.
The Meek is available to read online at www.meekcomic.com
this info section is called "indicia" btw, I hope you liked it~

THE MEEK

Volume 1

DER-SHING HELMER

This book is dedicated to you,
the person reading this comic.
Thank you for coming along
on this journey with me.

CHAPTER 1
lost and found

'SCUSE ME!

COME ON!

SHE WENT THIS WAY!

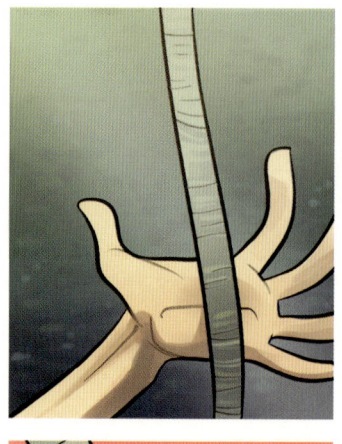

14

CHK!

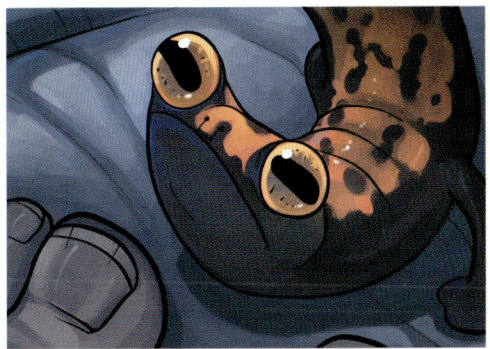

WHAT ARE YOU DOING UP SO LATE?

THINKIN' ABOUT THINGS?

YEAH, ME TOO.

OH!

HELLO!

CRACK

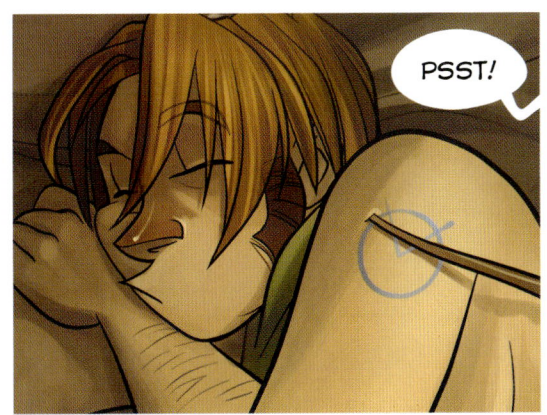

... SO! YOU'RE TRYING TO FIND YOUR GRAMPS.

YES! HE'S AT THE CENTER.

"DE" WHAT? "DESENTER?"

OH YEAH! THAT REMINDS ME, ARE YOU LOST?

UH

NO?

OH. THE LAST TIME I SAW MY GRANDFATHER, HE TOLD ME THAT-

"THE LOST ONE WILL KNOW THE WAY."

AND SINCE YOU HAVE THIS BIG MAP I THOUGHT MAYBE-

-YOU'D KNOW HOW TO GET TO THIS CITY!

SEE, LOOK! IT'S RIGHT AT THE CENTER OF EVERYTHING!

HEY, CUT IT OUT!

YOU- OKAY, *LOOK.* THIS IS THE CAPITAL, CITERAN.

LIKE YOU SAID, IT'S IN THE MIDDLE OF EVERYTHING. MOST ROADS LEAD TO IT.

YOU COULD HEAD NORTH ABOUT 80 MILES OVERLAND-

-OR YOU COULD TRY TO SNEAK ON TO ONE OF THOSE LUMBER SHIPS AND RIDE UP THE COAST. THAT'D BE THE FASTEST WAY.

SHIPS COME BY EVERY MONTH OR SO, AND THE PORT IS ONLY A MILE WEST OF HERE.

TELL ME WHICH WAY YOU'RE GOING SO I CAN GIVE YOU BETTER DIRECTIONS.

I THINK...

I'LL CHOOSE ...

WHY DON'T *YOU* TAKE ME?

FFT

27

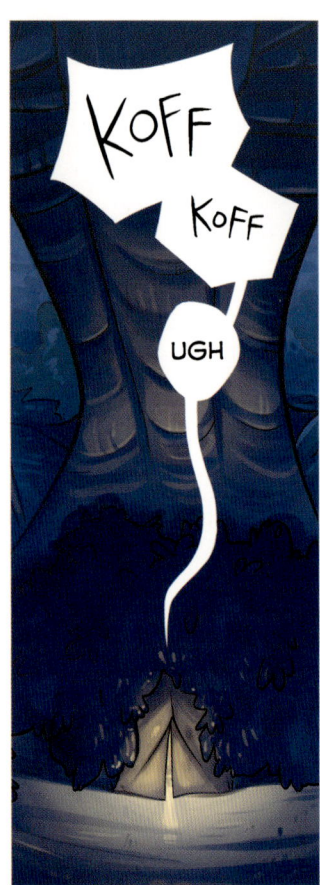

THAT'S RIGHT. *MOLDY.*

AND YOU HAVEN'T GOT ANY RESPECT FOR MY PERSONAL SPACE!

YES, I *DO!* AND MY HAIR IS *NOT* MOLDY!

IT'S *BEAUTIFUL,* AND IT CAN EVEN GROW FLOWERS IN THE SPRING!

THAT'S IT!

HERE!

GOING AWAY PRESENT!

!

THERE'S THE DOOR!

HEY!!

I HOPE YOU FIND YOUR GRANDPA AND GET SOME MENTAL HELP OR SOMETHING. GOODBYE!

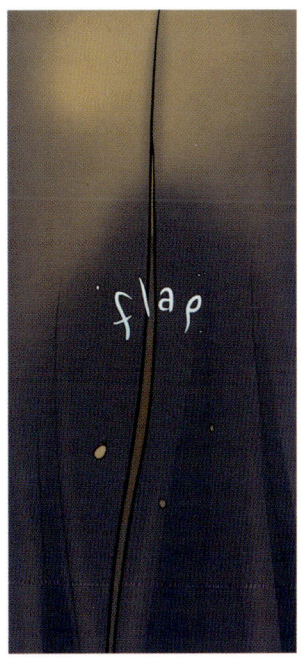

flap

WHY ARE YOU BEING SO MEAN?

GO AWAY!

BUT—

YOU HAVE THE MAP!

WHO ELSE AM I SUPPOSED TO ASK?

I DON'T *CARE!*

NOW FOR THE LAST TIME: GET THE HELL

OUT

OF

MY

TENT!

FINE! I'LL FIND MY OWN WAY!

AND I'M NOT GOING TO GIVE YOU YOUR STUPID STINKY WATER BACK EITHER!

31

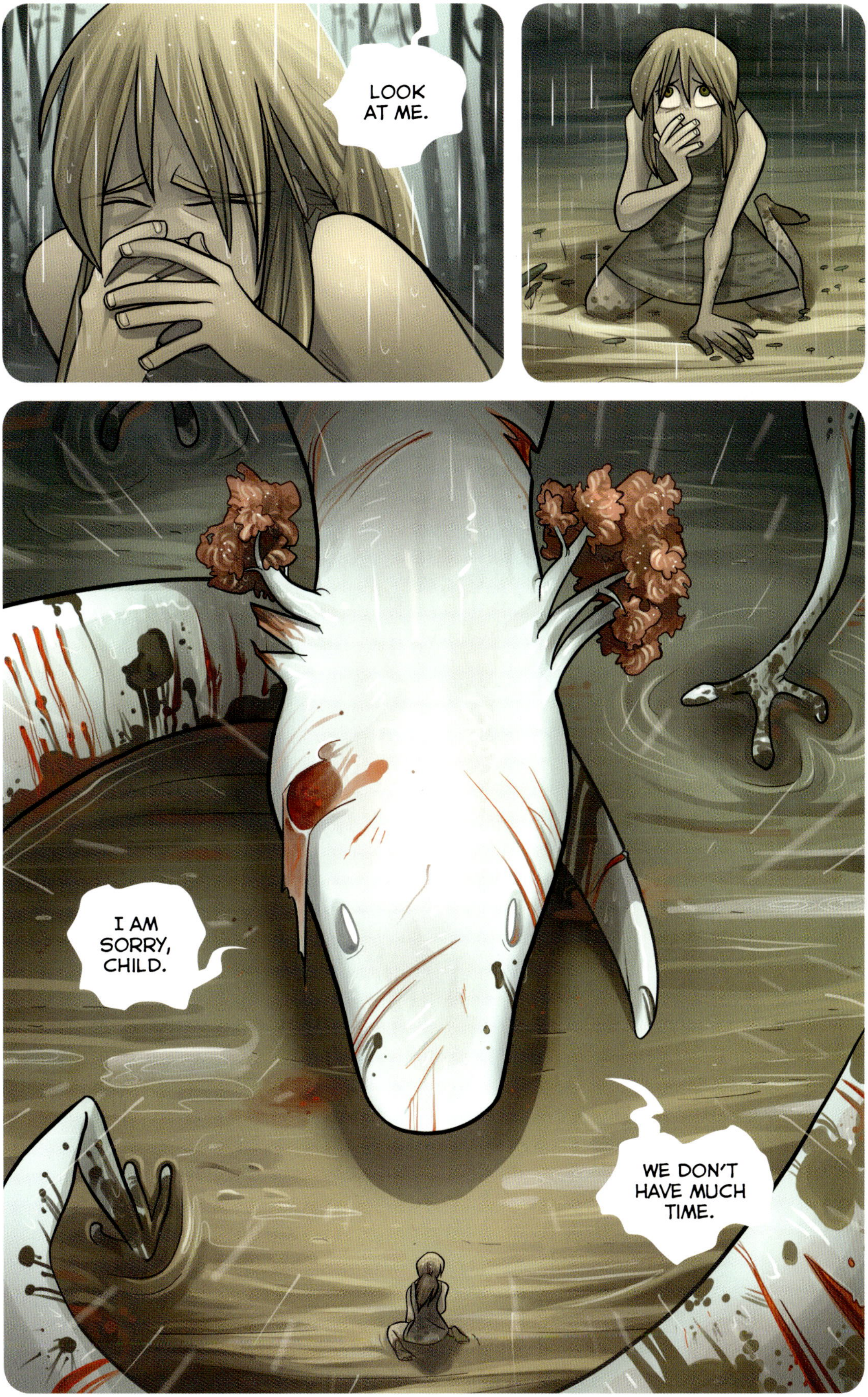

WHY, GRANDFATHER?

WHY WOULD ANYONE DO THIS TO YOU?

IT WAS MY BROTHER, ANGORA.

I NEARLY KILLED HIM, BUT I FAILED TO STOP HIM.

BECAUSE OF MY WEAKNESS HE IS RUSHING

USING THE LAST OF HIS STRENGTH

TO DESTROY YOUR PEOPLE FOREVER.

BUT *WHY?*

WHY WOULD HE DO THAT?

THIS STORY IS TOO LONG; THE TIME TOO SHORT.

I MUST LEAVE NOW IF I AM TO HAVE ANY CHANCE AT STOPPING HIM.

NO! YOU CAN'T! PLEASE

LISTEN! I NEVER WANTED TO SAY THESE WORDS TO YOU, CHILD.

BUT I NEED YOUR HELP.

38

STILL IN HIS TENT, NO LESS!

LET *GO!*

WH- WHAT ARE YOU DOING?

IS THAT MY RUCKSACK? AND MY *MAP??*

YOU WEREN'T USING THEM!

OW!

WHAT A SURPRISE, YOU FAT LIAR. SO YOU GET LOST, SCREW UP YOUR STUPID EXPEDITION, AND TOP IT OFF BY HANGING AROUND OUR CAMP? LEECHING OFF OUR SUPPLIES? STEALING OUR GIRLS??

LOST?

THEY CUT MY PAY! HOW FAIR IS THAT?

SO, PLEASE BELIEVE ME WHEN I SAY THAT YOU AIN'T GONNA BE POKING YOUR BIG BROWN NOSE AROUND HERE AGAIN.

AND I'M GONNA TAKE IT JUST TO MAKE SURE!

SO, JUST DO AS I SAY AND EVERYTHING WILL BE-

...

WHAT THE-

SHAK!

!!

STOP FIGHTING!

THIS'LL ONLY TAKE A SECOND.

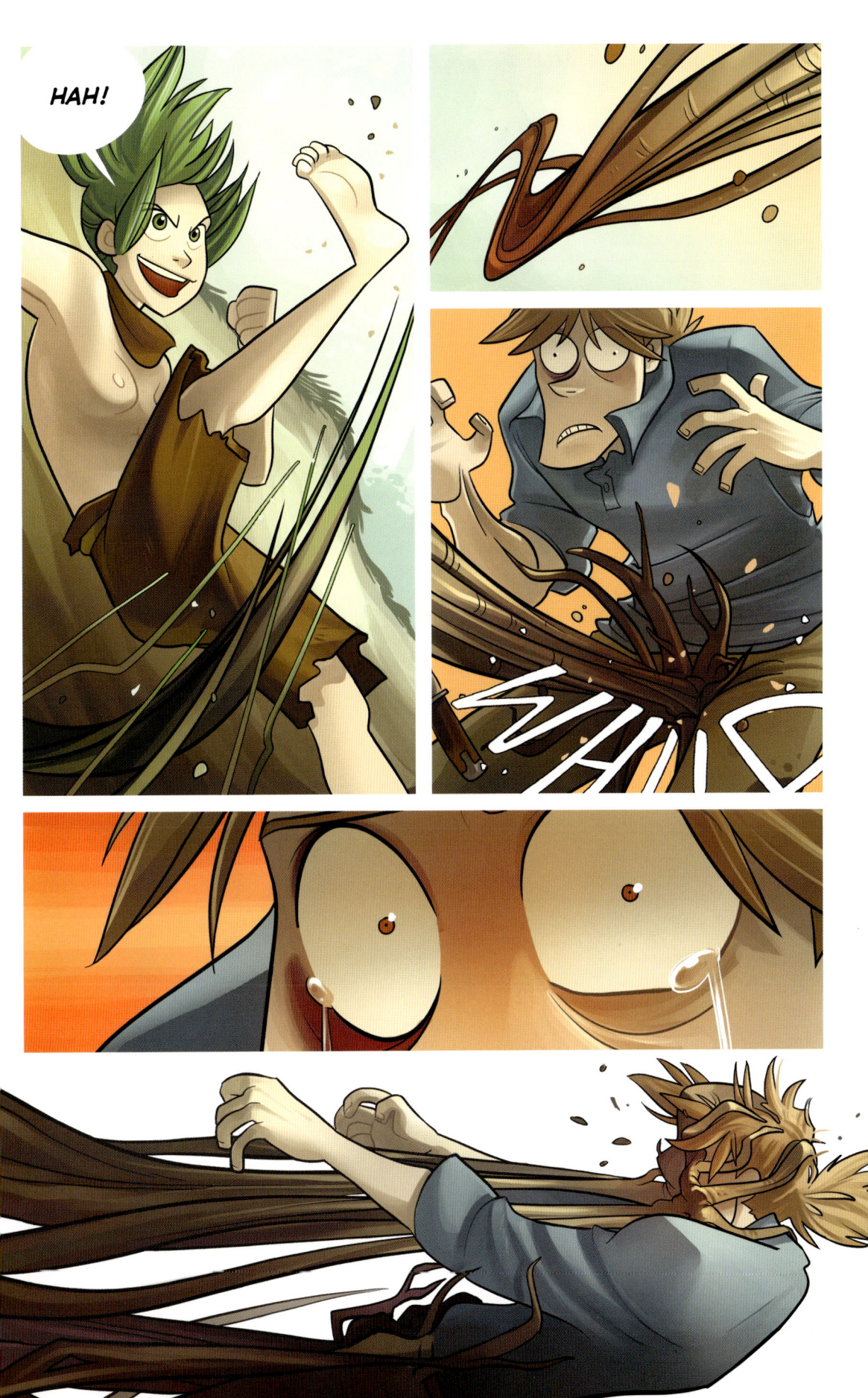

HELLO?

ARE YOU GONNA HELP ME?

NO!

I JUST DON'T WANT US TO GET OUR ASSES KICKED.

WHERE'S MY BAG?

OVER THERE.

HOW COME YOU DIDN'T TELL ME YOU WERE LOST?

WHY DO YOU KEEP ASKING ME THAT? I'M *NOT* LOST.

CHAPTER 2
the lady
and the tiger

YOU AREN'T THINKING ABOUT THE LONG TERM.

DON'T BE RIDICULOUS. THE LONG TERM IS ALL I THINK ABOUT.

THEN WHAT IS THE PROBLEM? ALL THEY WANT IS A PEACEFUL EXCHANGE.

THERE IS NOT A PROBLEM.

I HAVE NOTHING AGAINST PEACE.

I *LIKE* PEACE!

PHE, THEY NEARLY DESTROYED ALL OF OUR LIVES.

DO YOU TRULY TRUST THEM NOT TO TRY AGAIN, IF I GRANT TO THEM YOUR ALLOWANCES?

EXCUSE ME, "MY" WHA—

DO YOU WANT OUR CHILDREN TO SUFFER AS WE HAVE SUFFERED?

I HAVE MADE MY DECISION, AND IT IS FINAL.

I DO NOT NEED YOUR INPUT, AND I DO NOT NEED YOUR HELP!

...

THANKS.

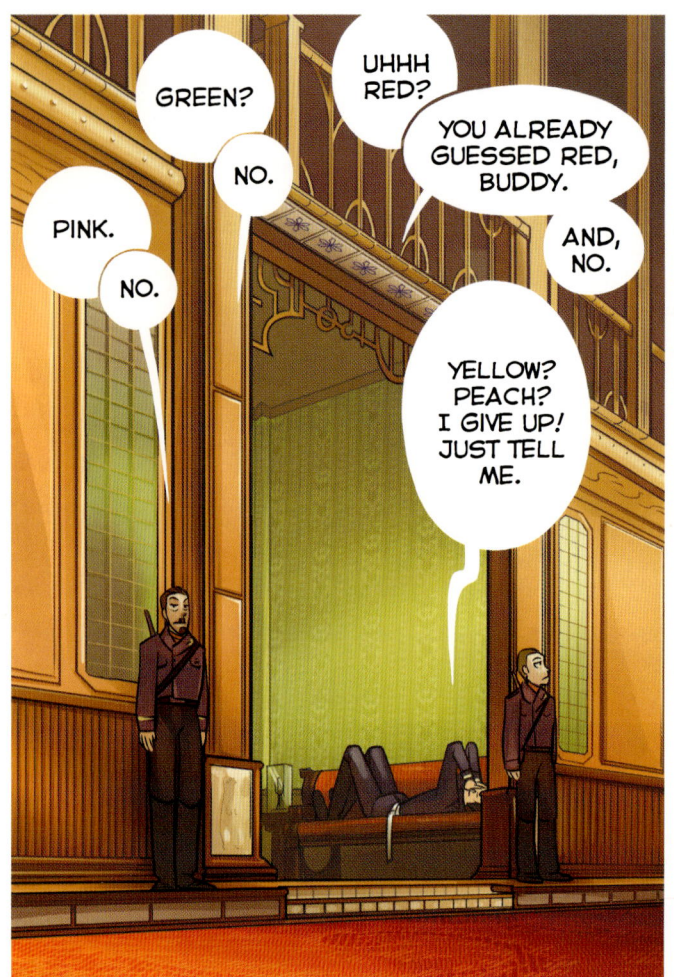

SON
OF THE
BEAR-

ENOUGH!

WHAT ARE
YOU HERE
FOR.

AMBASSADOR
TESA ALOVAN.

AMBASSADOR
LETHY ARAY!

WE WOULD LIKE TO
EXTEND THANKS ON THE BEHALF
OF THE COUNTRY OF CARIS FOR
YOUR MOST KIND ATTENDANCE
HERE TODAY.

OUR
QUEEN
EXPRESSES
REGRET FOR
NOT BEING
ABLE TO
PERS-

MY
QUESTION
WAS:

WHAT
ARE
YOU
HERE
FOR.

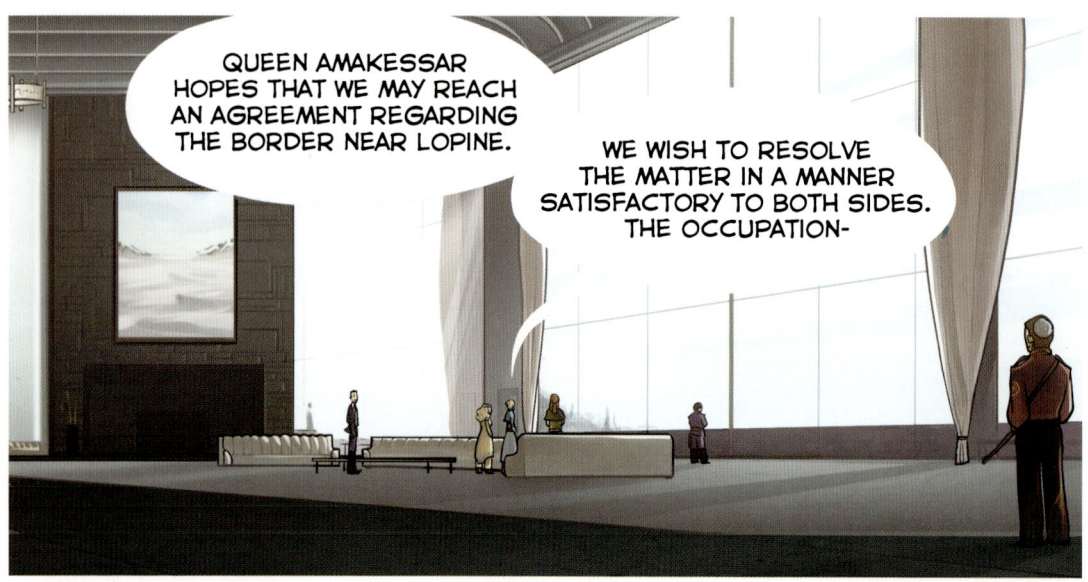

QUEEN AMAKESSAR HOPES THAT WE MAY REACH AN AGREEMENT REGARDING THE BORDER NEAR LOPINE.

WE WISH TO RESOLVE THE MATTER IN A MANNER SATISFACTORY TO BOTH SIDES. THE OCCUPATION-

LOPINE?

TAKE IT.

BORDER FORCES AS WELL, I WILL MOVE THEM FOR YOU.

MY COUNTRY AND MY PEOPLE WANT ONLY ONE THING FROM YOUR QUEEN:

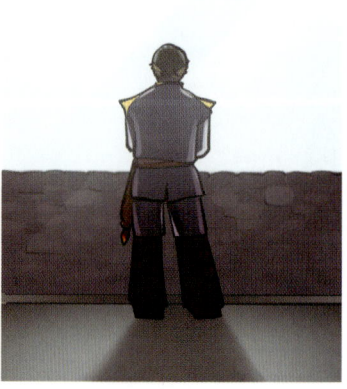

REPARATIONS.

SIR, THE QUEEN WISHES TO LET HER DEEPEST REGRETS ABOUT HER FATHER'S WAR BE KNOWN.

AS YOU KNOW, HIS DEATH BROUGHT ABOUT ITS END, AND BOTH SIDES SUFFERED DEAR LOSSES.

BUT WITH ALL DUE RESPECT...

CARIS IS SIMPLY UNABLE TO PROVIDE REPARATIONS FOR AMAKESSAR IV'S DECREES.

QUEEN SYMON WISHES TO FURTHER CLARIFY THAT SHE WILL NOT ACCEPT RESPONSIBILITY FOR ANY DEEDS ENACTED DURING THE COURSE OF HER FATHER'S WAR.

SO, NOBODY IS RESPONSIBLE.

MILLIONS DEAD, AND NOBODY IS RESPONSIBLE!

WITH RESPECT, THE QUEEN WISHES TO KNOW—

—WHY YOU INSIST ON HOLDING HER ACCOUNTABLE FOR DECISIONS MADE SOLELY BY HER FATHER?

WITH RESPECT, AMBASSADOR.

YOUR KING ALONE DID NOT UPHOLD AN ENTIRE COUNTRY'S INSTITUTION OF TORTURE AND MURDER AGAINST MY PEOPLE.

EMPEROR, SURELY-

THIS DISCUSSION IS OVER.

I GRANT YOU *NOTHING.* IN FACT, I WILL SEE THAT YOU-

-JOIN US AT DINNER TONIGHT.

ATDA??

IT WOULD BE PREMATURE FOR EITHER PARTY TO REACH A DECISION IN A SINGLE MEETING.

I AM CERTAIN THAT MY HUSBAND DID NOT MEAN TO ENCOURAGE SUCH HASTY DISCOURSE

!

PERHAPS IF BOTH SIDES WOULD AGREE TO FURTHER-

EXCUSE ME!

MY WIFE FORGETS HER PLACE! WHEN THE EMPEROR SPEAK

YOU DO NOT TO TALK ME LIKE-

WHEN THE EMPEROR STOP ACTING LIKE AN ANGRY *CHILD,* I WOULD BE MORE THAN-

...

yawn

AAAND THAT'S WHEN THEY KICKED ME OUT!

SO THEN I WENT TO THE KITCHEN.

...

ARE YOU *SERIOUS?*

HE BLEW UP IN FRONT OF EVERYONE?

THAT'S SO...

I MEAN...

WHERE'S MOM NOW? AND WHAT ABOUT THE AMBASSADORS?

MM.

DUNNO.

UGH! WHAT'S YOUR PROBLEM? DON'T YOU CARE ABOUT WHAT'S GOING ON?

GIVE ME SOME CREDIT, RANA.

I'LL BREAK IT DOWN.

DAD'S GONE CRAZY AGAIN,

MOM'S PISSED,

BOTH THE AMBASSADORS ARE HIDING,

AND DINNER MAY OR MAY NOT BE HAPPENING TONIGHT.

EITHER WAY, WE'RE NOT INVITED.

COOKIE?

... YOU *KNOW* I'M ON A DIET, SUDA.

WHATEVER, YOU'RE ALWAYS ON A DIET.

AND THESE ARE SOOOOO GOOOOD...

YOU'RE AN ASS.

HEY, WHERE ARE YOU GOING?

TO CHECK ON MOM, YOU *KNOB!*

OH, SHE'S *FINE.*

YOU KNOW THEY'RE JUST GOING TO SCREAM AT EACH OTHER AND THROW STUFF AND MAKE UP.

THEY ALWAYS DO.

BUT THEY DON'T FIGHT IN PUBLIC...

I JUST WANT TO MAKE SURE EVERYTHING IS OKAY.

I'LL SEE YOU LATER.

BRING BACK FOOD!

GOOD EVENING, PRINCESS RANA!

EVENING. I AM GOING IN TO SPEAK WITH MY MOTHER.

I'M SORRY, PRINCESS, YOUR FATHER SAYS HE IS NOT TO BE DISTURBED!

IF YOU WILL KINDLY COME BACK LATE-

ER

-

RIGHT.

TCH!

Click

CRASH!

TINKLE

69

PHE?

LETHY, I CAN'T *STAND* THIS PLACE.

THAT MAN IS A LUNATIC!

ALL OF THEM! JUST... BLOOD-DRINKING, CANNIBAL *LUNATICS!*

‹KEEP YOUR VOICE DOWN! AND SPEAK CARISSI, IF YOU LOVE THE QUEEN.›

‹RIGHT, SORRY...›

‹WE CAN WORK WITH THE WIFE.›

‹AND ANYHOW, DIDN'T YOU KNOW IT WAS GOING TO BE THIS WAY?›

‹OF COURSE I DID.›

‹JUST DIDN'T KNOW WE'D HAVE TO *EAT* WITH THEM.›

...

knock knock

LADY DESADAR!

PLEASE, JUST "PHE" IS FINE.

I'M HERE TO ESCORT YOU TO DINNER.

YOU ARE FAR TOO KIND.

NOT AT ALL.

THE EMPEROR HAS EATEN OF EVERY DISH.

BOTH FOOD AND HOST ARE PROVEN TRUSTWORTHY.

EAT IN HONOR OF YOUR EMPEROR.

...

CLINK

YOU'RE IN MY WA

I'LL MOVE WHEN YOU GET YOUR ELBOW OU OF MY FACE!

SLAM

JUST

...

WELL?

WHAT ARE YOU WAITING FOR?

THESE LITTLE BOYS HAVE NO SKILLS.

WHY SHOULD WE WASTE OUR GOOD PASORI STOCK ON POINTLESS SKIRMISHES?

WHO DO WE USE, THEN?

SANTRI?

THEY ARE SOFT AND UNBLOODED. I WOULDN'T TRUST THEM WITH MY LAUNDRY.

EASY FOR YOU TO SAY!

YOU DON'T GET UP FROM YOUR DESK UNLESS YOU HAVE TO TAKE A SHIT.

HA! HA!

BAS.

I'VE DONE MY SHARE OF FIGHTING.

I WOULDN'T DISGRACE OUR FINE ARMY BY SUGGESTING TH YOU REENLIST!

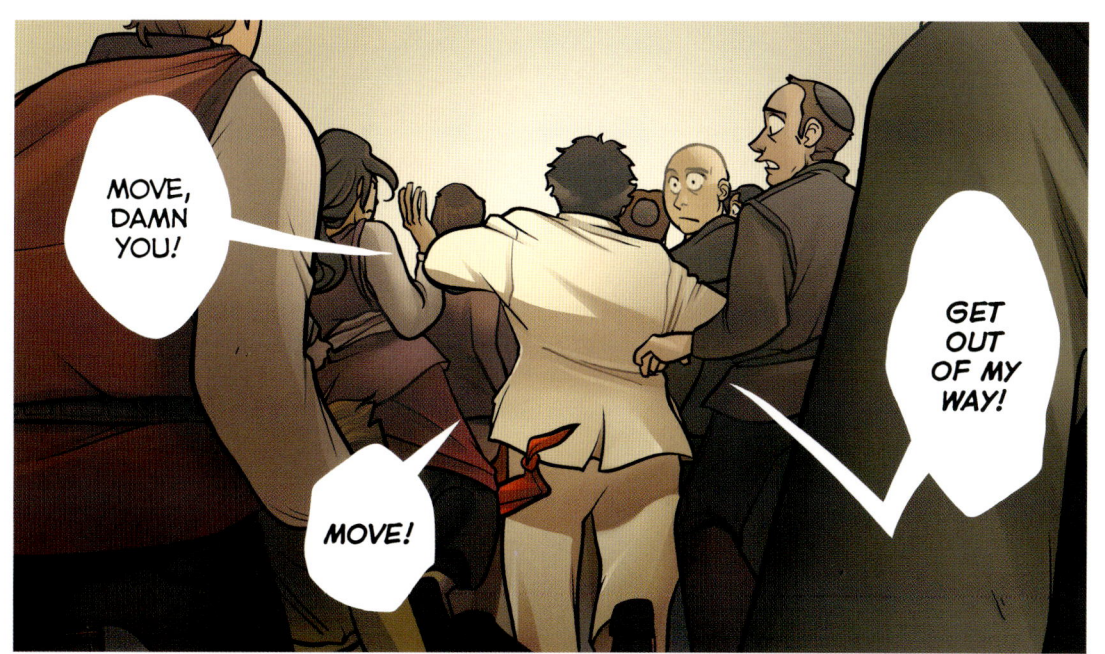

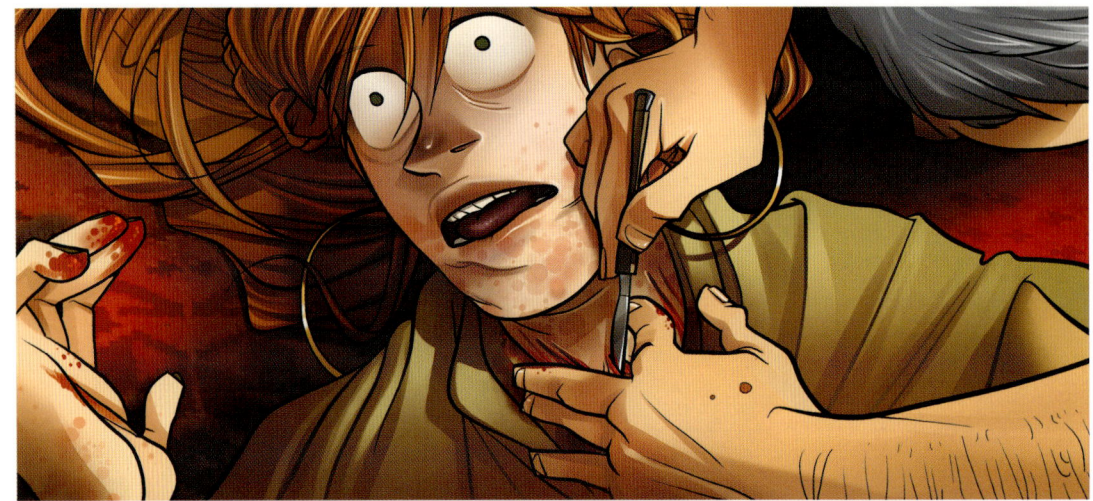

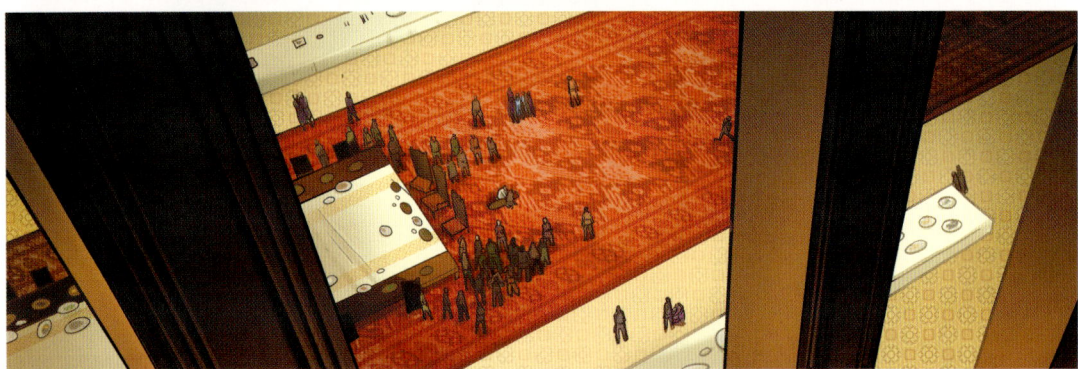

SIR?

SIR?

93

95

DOES HYLA...?

KNOW?

NO.

UNLESS YOU TOLD HER.

NO, I HAVEN'T HAD A CHANCE TO SEE HER.

AND DAD'S LOCKED HIM- SELF IN HIS CHAMBERS...

DAD?

RANA, WHAT'S HE GONNA DO WITHOUT HER?

WHAT ARE *WE* GONNA DO?

I JUST DON'T UNDERSTAND!

WHY WOULD ANYONE WANT TO HURT HER?

OH

I THINK I MIGHT HAVE AN IDEA.

CHAPTER 3
water in
the desert

HUH.

WHAT'RE YOU DOING?

GAH!

I DO?

YOU CAN'T JUST COME AND TAKE MY WORK FROM ME!

THIS RESEARCH STATION, IT REPRESENTS A DECADE'S WORTH OF EFFORT!

BETTER YOU THAN ME.

WHAT GIVES YOU THE RIGHT TO COME HERE AND DESTROY TEN YEARS OF MY LIFE?

DON'T BE SO DRAMATIC, GRANPA.

IT'S NOT LIKE WE'RE CHOPPING YOUR LEG OFF; IT'S JUST A COUPLE OF BOOKS.

YOU CAN GET MORE.

MORE?

MORE?

MORE OF MY RESEARCH NOTES? WHERE DO YOU THINK THEY COME FROM?

AND THE BOOKS ARE ON LOAN FROM THE ROYAL LIBRARY! SOME OF THESE ARE THE ONLY COPIES IN EXISTENCE!

ARE YOU REALLY IGNORANT THAT

WELL, HEY! IF THEY'RE SO DAMNED IMPORTANT, MAYBE THEY SHOULDN'T HAVE LOANED THEM OUT TO SOME CRAZY IDIOT LIVING BY HIMSELF IN THE MIDDLE OF THE DESERT!

SO SHUT UP ALREADY!

113

SIR, YOU ARE BEING ARRESTED FOR THE ASSAULT OF A ROYAL OFFI-

GOOD LORD.

YOU'RE A *WOMAN?*

PST.

PST!

SOLI!

YEAH?

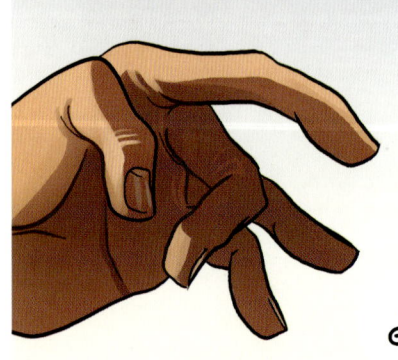

-JUST WANT YOU TO KNOW THAT I'M REAL SORRY ABOUT...

ALL THIS.

WHY'D YOU HAVE TO FIGHT? I WOULD'VE LET YOU GO.

YOU GOT A ROSARY OR SOMETHING?

NNH!

NNH!

NNH!

...

ALRIGHT, WHAT?

IN THE NAME OF HER HOLY HIGHNESS THE PRINCEPS SYMON, I HEREBY PLACE YOU UNDER ARREST!

THE FACT IS, ALI

YOU DON'T KNOW WHEN TO SHUT UP.

WROONG

NO, I'M SERIOUS.

YOU NEED TO WATCH WHAT COMES OUT OF YOUR MOUTH.

WELL, IT'S YOUR FAULT TOO!

YOU SHOULDN'TVE HIT ME IN FRONT OF TWO GUYS!

ONE OF THEM WASN'T EVEN AWAKE.

SOLI, IT...

IT'S ABOUT THE PRINCIPLE.

YOU KIDS BEEN UNDER A ROCK?

SOME TOWHEADS MURDERED THE EMPEROR'S WIFE.

THEY LOCKED THE BORDER LAST NIGHT.

REALLY?!?

SHIT.

ONLY WAY IN NOW IS THROUGH ME.

...

IT'LL BE OKAY ONCE WE'RE IN.

ALI, YOU *SWEAR* YOU'RE SURE ABOUT YOUR GUY.

100 PERCENT!

FINE.

TAKE THEM.

BYE, SALLY.

COME ON, BUDDY.

OKAY, HERE WE ARE.

HEY, LET US IN!

PASSWORD?

DOG BUTTS!

NOPE, THAT'S THE OLD PASSWORD.

HUH?

YEAH, WE CHANGED IT LAST WEEK.

WELL, WHAT THE HECK AM I S'PPOSED TO DO NOW?

UH... GUESS?

CAT BUTTS?

NO.

DONKEY BUTTS?

NOPE.

FACE BUTTS?

WHAT?

UH... BUTTSMELL?

OOH, CLOSE.

BUTT SMELLING.

BUTTSMELLER!

I STINK LIKE A SEWER, I'M CARRYING 70 POUNDS OF CONTRABAND ON MY BACK, AND I JUST GAVE AWAY A SMALL FORTUNE IN HORSES.

I AM *NOT* IN A HAPPY MOOD.

SO YOU'RE GOING TO OPEN THIS DOOR *RIGHT NOW* OR BY GOD I'M GOING TO MAKE YOU WISH YOU HAD.

YEAH.

DEFINITELY WOULDN'TVE GUESSED THAT.

LISTEN, I DUNNO IF IT'S A GOOD IDEA TO LET HER IN HERE...

WHY? YOU GOT SOMETHING AGAINST MY GIRLFRIEND?

YOUR-

...

SO WHAT'S THIS THING ABOUT THE EMPEROR?

OH YEAH, I GUESS SOME CARISSI OFFED HER?

NEXT THING YOU KNOW THERE'S PATROLS EVERYWHERE, AND EVERYONE'S GOIN' CRAZY...

IT'S A GOOD THING YOU GUYS GOT SOMETHIN' OUT THOUGH, GOODS FROM CARIS ARE GONNA BE WORTH A LOT SOON.

WHAT DO YOU MEAN?

YOU KNOW, AFTER THE EMPEROR DECLARES WAR?

BOSS, COMIN' IN!

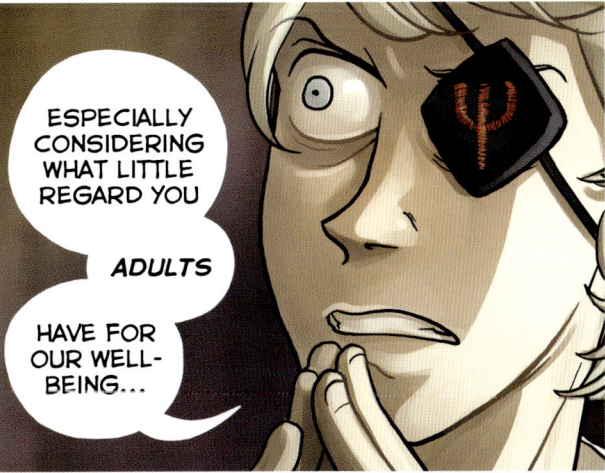

COUGH

OOPS!

RIGHT! WHAT DID YOU BRING ME?

HEAVY! ARE THESE BRICKS OR BOOKS?

WHAT'S THIS?

IT'S A... UH, THING.

IT MAKES NOISE.

THAT'S GOOD!

NOISE IS VERY, VERY GOOD.

I'LL GIVE YOU FIVE FOR IT.

FIVE? ARE YOU *NUTS?* I BUSTED MY ASS FOR THESE.

WE'RE NOT EVEN TALKIN' FOR LESS THAN TWO THOU.

YOU'RE NOT VERY GOOD AT THIS.

THAT'S FIVE *THOUSAND.*

WE'RE NOT EVEN TALKING TO YOU FOR LESS THAN TEN THOU—

DON'T.

I GUARANTEE YOU, NOBODY PAYS HIG[H] FOR RELICS TH[AT]

WE'LL TAKE IT.

WONDERFUL!

I'D ALSO APPRECIATE IF YOU WOULD BRING FUTURE ACQUISITIONS TO ME FIRST.

WE'RE NOT-

JUST. KEEP IT IN MIND.

BY THE WAY, YOU'LL WANT TO BE CAREFUL OUT THERE.

I HEAR THE PATROLS ARE BECOMING MORE AGGRESSIVE.

SHE DOESN'T HAVE T' WORRY!

I'M LOOKIN' OUT FOR HER.

WE'RE GETTIN' MARRIED YOU KNOW.

...

UHHHH.

CONGRATS?

SERIOUSLY, YOU NEED TO SHUT UP.

SHOULDN'T A MAN BRAG ABOUT HIS WOMAN?

ALI, THIS IS IT, THIS IS ENOUGH! WE-

SOLDIERS!

BOSS!

BOSS!!

HEY!

THEY'RE *RAIDING!*

WHAT?

HOW DID THEY...

IT'S NOT JUST US!

SOLDIERS ARE GOIN' UP AN' DOWN ALL THE ALLEYS.

THEY'RE TAKIN' TOWHEADS!

...

TOM, PLEASE GATHER EVERYONE ON THE GROUND FLOOR AND TAKE THEM TO THE BYPASS.

I'LL GET THIS FLOOR.

WE CAN LEAVE ALL THE GOODS HERE! THEY'RE WORTH

NOW, TOM.

Y-YES BOSS!

YOU TWO!

TAKE ALL THE KIDS AND GET OUT!

GO!

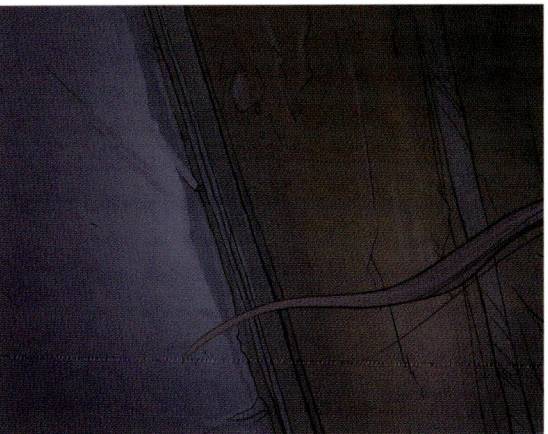

142

143

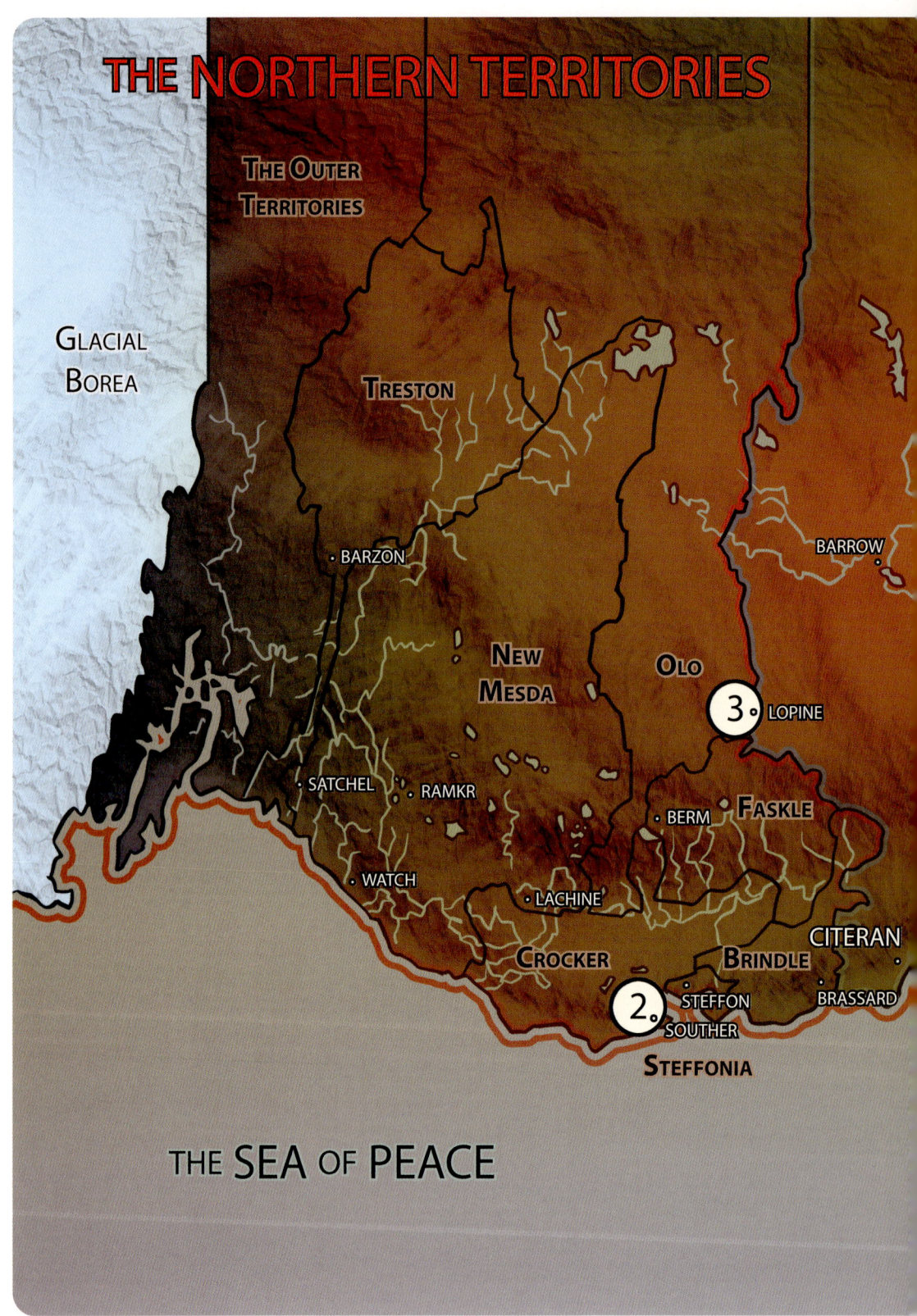

MAP OF DIA

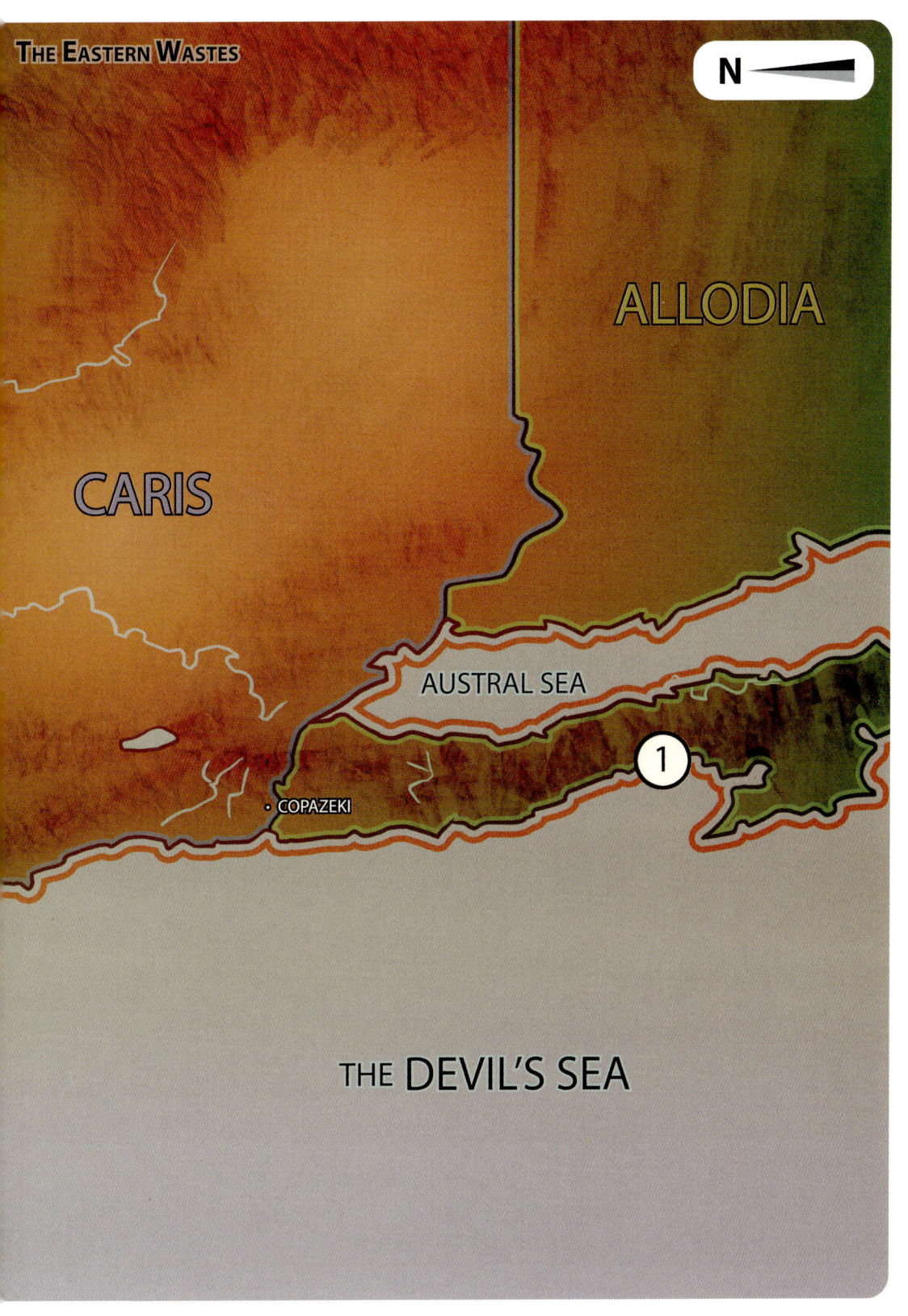

THE EASTERN WASTES

N

ALLODIA

CARIS

AUSTRAL SEA

①

· COPAZEKI

THE DEVIL'S SEA

1. ROYAL LOGGING COMAPNY CAMP, ALLODIA
2. SOUTHER PALACE, THE TERRITORIES
3. LOPINE, CARIS

CARIS: COUNTRY OF LIGHT

The capitol city of Caris, Citeran, is highly recognizable for its golden dome.

Caris is the southernmost country in Dia, also referred to as the "Land of Light" or "Land of Enlightenment." The region borders the Northern Territories to the north and the densely forested Allodia region to the south. Although it comprises roughly the same amount of area as the Territories, most of Caris is uninhabited desert, with the bulk of the population concentrated along the coast. Its most famous city, the coastal capital of Citeran, is well known for being a hub of sea and overland transportation as well as commerce. The capitol is also seat to the monarchy of the Amakessar dynasty, which ruled for several hundred years prior to the Dark Years, and continues to maintain power till this day through the Princeps Symon Amakessar. Caris as a country is inextricable from Caris as a religion; the monarchy and the religious text of the Invidgeon were said to be divinely appointed, and subject to no mortal authority.

Caris is made up of two major ethnic groups: the Carissi and the "Southern" Santri. The Carissi, who consider themselves indigenous to the region, are easily identifiable by their predominately light hair and complexions, as well as a generally lighter build. The Southern Santri by comparison are early migrants from the (now dissolved) country of Old Mesda, and are overwhelmingly converts from Generalism to the ubiquitous Carissi religion. For an unknown reason, likely interracial mixing, most southern transplants have an unpigmented nose, but have retained the darker hair and more robust features more typical of northerners.

A Carissi girl

In recent history, Caris has been beset by many challenges both internal and external. Following the end of the Thirty Year's War and the death of Furano Amakessar IV, much of the country was thrust into turmoil with the ascension of the first female to the throne. Many still fear that this will have dire consequences, and rifts are already beginning to form within the church. Additionally, the Northern Territories under the leadership of Emperor deSadar have continued to demand reparations for an earlier period of human trafficking that the country is ill-able to afford. With a new international conflict building, it seems very likely that more upheaval is on the way.

THE NORTHERN TERRITORIES

The Northern Territories, often shortened to "the Territories," are the eight united states made up of the dissolved country of Old Mesda, and the region previously categorized as "Borea," which is now simply referred to as the Outer Territories. The Northern Territories were formed after the end of the Thirty Years War in HY727 under the leadership of Emperor Luca deSadar (formerly Sadr) of the Pasori Gulo tribe. Emperor deSadar still maintains power over the territories as de facto leader, but is widely considered at home and abroad to be a dictator.

A statue of Emperor deSadar

Old Mesda was once the largest country in the world by population, and home to a mix of Santri citizens and immigrants from Caris. The republic of Old Mesda was well-known for its forays into industrialization and emphasis on a free economy. Some popular innovations of the hundreds of years of Old Mesda's existence include the modern printing press, the modern steam automobile, and the "Swaft" music fad which is still enjoyed to this day. Due to language barriers and the insular nature of the Pasori people, the Santri of Old Mesda did not initially maintain a great deal of contact with the tribes of Lower Borea, but in the 600's did expand their outreach to a minimal degree (although a path to full citizenship did not exist until wartime in the 700's).

The Borea region is comprised of the lands of the Upper and Lower tribes, now called the Outer Territories, but still made up of roughly the same area. Borea was once considered to be completely uninhabitable; the Lower regions are distinguished from the Upper by whether or not the ground ever thaws during the course of the year. The uppermost tribes are adapted to life in the permanently snow-covered forests or the frigid plateaus. Due to a lack of resources, tribes are deeply protective of their boundaries, and have earned a reputation for being starved, ravenous, and literally bloodthirsty. In reality, the tribes do engage in warfare fairly frequently, but have also been known to convene to form alliances during especially difficult environmental or political circumstances. However, tribes have gone extinct—most famously the "extinct" tribe of the Pasori Ar, whose enslavement and genocide triggered the war between Mesda and Caris.

The extant Territories exist in a balance never before seen: a successful integration of the Pasori and Santri peoples in response to the external threat of southern aggression. Despite criticisms about the Emperor's methods of staying in power, many agree that no other man could have closed the gap between the societies of Mesda and the frozen north. Whether this balance can be maintained in light of devastating recent events remains to be seen.

The Emperor's late wife stamped into currency

Allodia, meaning literally "below Dia," is an area of unknown size that extends below the borders of Caris. The region is covered in a tropical rainforest that has never been fully penetrated nor mapped; the forest hides several bodies of water of unknown size, old settlements, and abandoned military installations. Due to the difficulty of traveling through the jungles, it is mostly only visited by Carissi prison laborers, logging and mining operations, and sometimes a mix of the two. Several expeditions have been carried out to fully map the area, but most have ended in failure or tragedy.

The RMC and RLC are a familiar presence in the jungle

In the latter years of the Thirty Years War, newly conscripted troops—mostly naïve young men of Borea hoping to earn permanent citizen status in Mesda after the war—were shipped to Allodia to follow the main body of the retreating Carissi army. An estimated 90% of these untrained ground troops were killed in action, died of disease and even starvation when weak supply chains were broken. Mass graves are still unearthed regularly.

Molio, a popular fruit

Despite its bloody history and the dangers inherent to the wilderness, Allodia is rich in resources, and is a great boon to Caris and its economy. Precious metals found in Allodia include silver, gold, zinc and copper, all of which are mined by the RMC. Additionally, prized hardwoods are regularly logged for use in construction and furniture-making. The jungle is also home to a variety of species with a wide range of culinary and medicinal uses. Due to the poor soil, farming and agriculture in this area is not often utilized, but more and more acreage is cleared every year to accommodate Caris's rebounding population.

A rectangular depression which forms after a rain often signals the location of a mass grave

Allodia is perhaps the gateway to the future of Dia, not just for its known natural bounty, but for the secrets that it continues to hide from the civilized world. As tensions rise in the cities, more and more individuals seek out an escape from the stress of modern life and have created an alternative far away from the hubs of society. Old buildings, once abandoned are being renovated and rebuilt by fringe groups hoping to regain their connection to a more peaceful lifestyle. And, alluringly, there is some indication of habitation further south, far beyond any known settlements of Dia. Time will tell if the forest will reveal these secrets, or if it will continue to keep them to itself.